Clara and the Bossy

Ruth Ohi

Annick Press
Toronto ❀ New York ❀ Vancouver

We acknowledge the support of the Canada Council for the Arts, the Ontario Arts Council, and the Government of Canada through the Book Publishing Industry Development Program (BPIDP) for our publishing activities.

Cataloging in Publication

Ohi, Ruth
    Clara and the Bossy / written and illustrated by Ruth Ohi.

ISBN-13: 978-1-55037-943-3 (bound)
ISBN-10: 1-55037-943-7 (bound)
ISBN-13: 978-1-55037-942-6 (pbk.)
ISBN-10: 1-55037-942-9 (pbk.)

I. Title.

PS8579.H47C53 2006   jC813'.6   C2005-905715-7

The art in this book was rendered in watercolor.
The text was typeset in Cheltenham.

Distributed in Canada by: Published in the U.S.A. by:
Firefly Books Ltd.   Annick Press (U.S.) Ltd.
66 Leek Crescent   Distributed in the U.S.A. by:
Richmond Hill, ON   Firefly Books (U.S.) Inc.
L4B 1H1   P.O. Box 1338
                                 Ellicott Station
                                 Buffalo, NY 14205

Printed in China.

Visit us at: www.annickpress.com

For Anne Millyard, with gratitude.
—R.O.

In all the world there was only one Clara quite like Clara.

These are my bedtime friends — Fuzz, Fluff, and Stripe. Fuzz is kind of fuzzy, Fluff is kind of fluffy, and Stripe likes polka dots and being in the middle.

Clara loved purple.

She loved triangles.

She loved tuna sandwiches.

Clara loved it when a girl called Madison
came up to her and said, "Let's be best friends!"
"OK," said Clara.

Madison was the type of girl who always said "good morning" to all the teachers she saw. Clara was too shy to say anything unless she was spoken to first.

On Monday after school, Madison asked Clara over to her house. Her mom said that was fine.

Pretend that mine's Queen of the World and yours is the humble servant and pretend that yours gets sick and has to stay in bed and pretend that I go off on a mighty quest to find a cure...

Madison had many toys. They played with puzzles, books, dolls, robots, and a tea set that talked. At the end of the playdate, Madison's room was a mess.

"Clara," said Madison, "can you clean up, please? I'm way too tired!"

Clara tried her best to put things back in the right place. Madison helped.

On Tuesday, Madison asked, "Why do you always wear the same dress every day?"

Clara looked down at her dress. She did wear it a lot. It was her favorite. Her mom had sewn large pockets on the front so that Clara would have a place to store any treasures she found.

On Wednesday, Clara wore her yellow dress.

"Why do you always have tuna sandwiches?" asked Madison at lunchtime.

Clara looked at her sandwich. She loved tuna. Her mom put bits of pickle in it, which made it extra-yummy.

On Thursday, Clara brought a ham sandwich.

"Why are your sandwiches always cut in triangles?" asked Madison.

Clara liked triangles. She looked at Madison's sandwiches. There was one star, one heart, and one in the shape of a trotting moose.

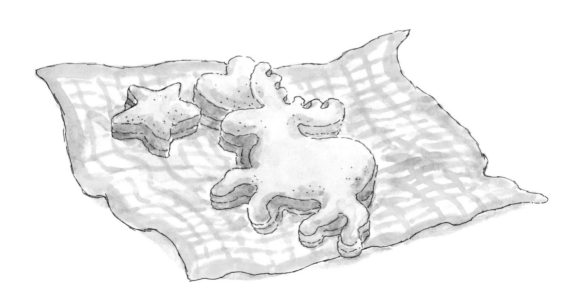

"Clara," said Madison, "will you open my milk, please? I don't want to break a nail."

Clara opened her friend's milk box and said, "Don't you miss out on a lot of things worrying about your nails?"

Madison sipped her milk daintily.

At recess, Clara found a perfectly round stone. It was purple and had tiny flecks of something that looked like stars. The yellow dress did not have pockets, so Clara tucked the stone into the cuff of her sleeve for safekeeping.

During art class, Clara looked for her treasure. It was gone.

"That's too bad," said Madison. "It must have fallen out. You should have asked me to hold it for you."

Madison turned to a boy
called Burt. "What's with you and
dinosaurs anyway?"
Burt blushed and bit his lip.

That night, Clara looked at her purple dress hanging in the closet.

She thought of the lost purple stone.

She thought of tuna and triangles.

She thought of dinosaurs.

On Friday, Clara wore her purple dress.
"You're wearing that dress again," said Madison.
"Yes, I like this dress," said Clara.
"Whatever," said Madison, and walked away.

At recess, Clara climbed the monkey bars.

At lunchtime, she ate tuna sandwiches that were cut in the shape of triangles.

On Saturday, Madison found Clara in the playground.

"I found Purple," said Madison. "They're for you, if you like."

"Thanks," said Clara. "Hey, Burt made a barosaurus in the sandbox. Do you want to come see?"

I made a swamp for it by flooding the sandbox !!!

Madison nodded shyly. "And, er ...
do you think that maybe, sometime,
I could try a triangle?"

"Sure," said Clara, smiling. "After
all, that's what friends are for!"

The barosaurus
was as tall as a five-
story building ...

Wow.

Cool.